Little Pig, Big Trouble

Told and illustrated by Eve Tharlet

PICTURE BOOK STUDIO

Translated by Andrew Clements

Midway between the woods above and the river below, there was a farmhouse, a small stone farmhouse with a big fireplace inside. Little Pierre lived here with his pig, Henri. Pierre and Henri were different, of course, but they were great friends.

They did everything together. They hunted for mushrooms together, they took long walks, they raced their scooters, and they fished in the river, always together. They even played bugle duets. But when it came to doing really silly, careless, foolish things, Henri worked alone.

It was Henri who painted a picture with the strawberry jam. It was Henri who made fancy costumes by cutting up the bedspread.
It was Henri who nearly burned the roof off the house. And it was Henri who invented dangerous games: pig-on-a-perch; leap-pig; little lost piggie; hopping-thunderpig... and little Pierre could do nothing about it.

Very early one morning, Henri went out of the house. He had nothing particular to do, so he began chasing a butterfly. He ran so fast and so far that before he knew it, he was at the edge of the town.

"Look! What a cute little dog," said a grandmother as she opened her shutters and looked around without putting on her glasses. "Come here, little poochie, and get yourself right into my house before you get into trouble!"

No sooner said than done:
Henri was not looking where he was
walking, and he slipped and slid right down
a coal chute, and completely disappeared into
a big pile of coal. He came out a moment later,
huffing and puffing and covered with black coal
dust, from the top of his flat little snout to the tip of
his curly tail.

Henri scrambled out of the cellar, and because he was
frightened, he ran off at top speed down the middle of
the main street. And there, coming straight at him, was
a big rattly old farm wagon. It was so huge and noisy
that Henri panicked and went charging through the open
door of the bakery, where the baker was making his bread
and dough.

And Henri, who had not even been properly introduced,
ran like a madman right through the dough that the
baker was kneading there in the trough, stomped on the
croissants, and then bumped smack into the unhappy fellow.
"What a monster!" he cried. "Aaagh! What dirt!" he bellowed.
As the baker reached for a board to whack this creature,
a huge sack tipped over on top of Henri,
and he scampered away in a white cloud of flour.

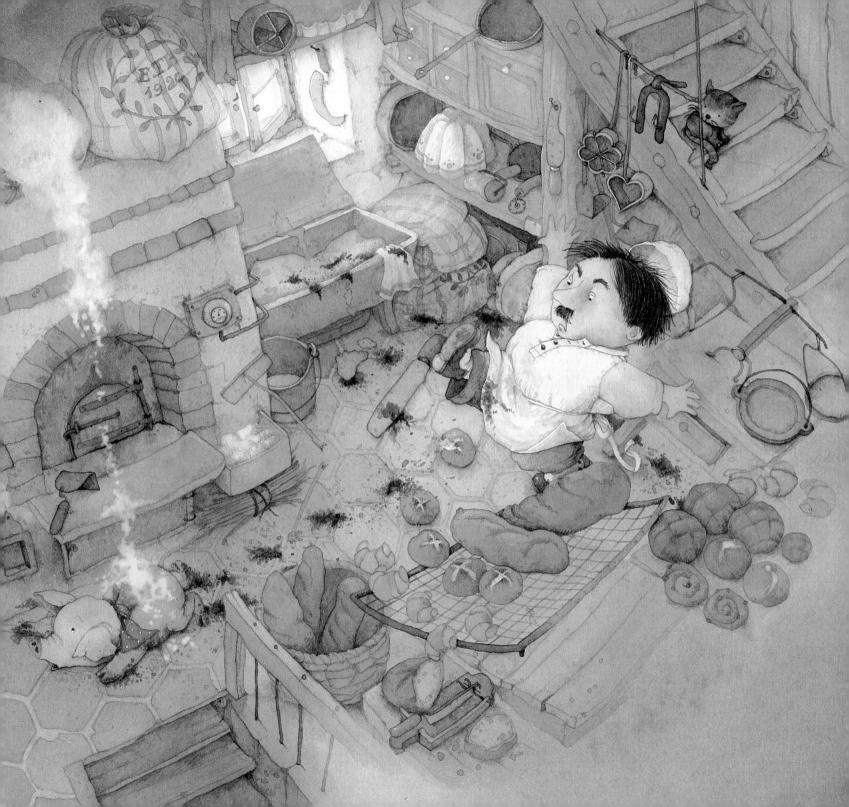

The baker chased Henri out into the street, but Henri quickly hid himself. The baker ran off to tell his story to the butcher, and then he told it to the seedsman, and then the grocer and the banker. Soon the whole town knew: "If that nasty black and white monster comes around again and tries to ruin my shop and get everthing all dirty, I am going to scream for the police!"

Henri shivered and sadly thought of little Pierre, who would certainly be worried about him by now. "I wish I was back home," he thought.

Henri crept out of his hiding place because
he wanted to slip away without being seen. But, of course, everybody
saw him and everybody chased him. As Henri ran past with the whole
town after him, everything was turned topsy turvy, and it looked like
a huge wind had blown the town to pieces.
Henri thought that he was getting away from the crowd, but then he
turned a corner, and ran right into a big scaffold. A huge bucket of blue
paint tipped off and splattered all over of him.

All this time, little Pierre was searching for his friend. After looking everywhere else, he came to the town. All he had to do was look and listen to figure out what was happening. There was an uproar coming from the direction of the little bridge which crossed the river, so Pierre ran off through the winding streets to investigate.

A crowd was there, and people were shouting and waving their arms.
"I've never seen anything like this before!" someone exclaimed.
"Such a creature, such nerve!" shouted another.
"I finally saw it – it was a dragon!" yelled a third.

Little Pierre came to the bridge as everyone else was leaving. There was nothing more to see but some tracks and some spots of black and white and blue. Henri had disappeared over the edge.

"He's drowned," wailed Pierre.
"I'll never see my Henri again."

Back home at the farm, Pierre went down by the river and just sat there, still crying. But suddenly there was a commotion out in the water.
And there in the distance Pierre saw Henri, holding onto a tree branch. In less time than it takes to say it, Pierre was hugging his friend. They laughed and laughed and laughed again.

Little Pierre got just as muddy and just as covered with colors as Henri, and as they walked uphill toward their house, the meadow of little white flowers got a good blue splashing.

Once they were all cleaned up,
Henri promised that he would never leave home again.
And he didn't.

And he also promised that he would never do anything
foolish again.
But he did.

A Michael Neugebauer Book
Copyright © 1989 Neugebauer Press, Salzburg, Austria.
Original title: "Henri, le petit cochon bleu"
Published and distributed in USA by Picture Book Studio, Saxonville, MA.
Distributed in Canada by Vanwell Publishing, St. Catharines, Ont.
Published in U.K. by Picture Book Studio, Neugebauer Press Ltd, London.
Distributed in U.K. by Ragged Bears, Andover.
Distributed in Australia by Era Publications, Adelaide.
All rights reserved.
Printed in Belgium by Proost.

LIBRARY OF CONGRESS CATALOGING IN PUBLICATION DATA
Tharlet, Eve
Little pig, big trouble / Eve Tharlet.
Translation of: Henri, le petit cochon bleu.
Summary: Little Pierre and Henri the pig are friends who enjoy
each other's company and do everything together but Henri has
a way of always getting into trouble.
ISBN 0-88708-073-1
[1. Pigs–Fiction, 2. Friendship–Fiction.] I. Title.
PZ7.T326Li   1989
[E] – dc19   89-31369

Ask your bookseller for these other PICTURE BOOK STUDIO books
illustrated by Eve Tharlet:
DIZZY FROM FOOLS by M. L. Miller
THE PRINCESS AND THE PEA by H.C. Andersen
THE WISHING TABLE by The Brothers Grimm
THE BRAVE LITTLE TAILOR by The Brothers Grimm

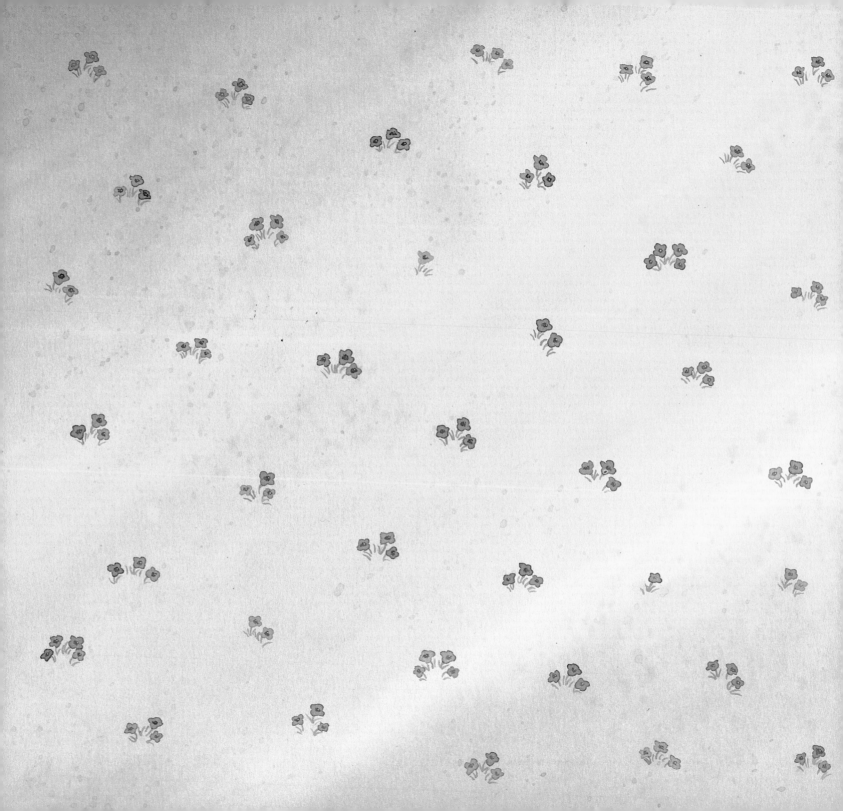